NEAT-O

T·H·E

SUPERMARKET
MOUSE

NEAT-O
T·H·E
SUPERMARKET MOUSE

TOM TICHENOR

**ILLUSTRATED BY
RAY CRUZ**

Abingdon • Nashville

Library of Congress Cataloging in Publication Data

Tichenor, Tom.
    Neat-O, the supermarket mouse.
    SUMMARY: A little mouse forsakes his daily bubble
bath in order to become part of the tough neighborhood
gang.
    [1.   Baths—Fiction.   2.   Mice—Fiction]
I.   Cruz, Ray.   II.   Title.
PZ7.T4335Ne   [E]   80-24770

ISBN 0-687-27690-X

NEAT-O THE SUPERMARKET MOUSE

MANUFACTURED IN THE UNITED STATES OF AMERICA

To

Felicia Fieldmouse

whose persistent neatness undoubtedly inspired this story

The front of Superservice Supermarket was a busy place. There were people rushing in and out all the time. Shopping carts stood in bunches by the front doors.

Behind the supermarket, the big trucks unloaded all the things sold inside, and empty boxes and trash were dumped there.

There were boxes with wilted vegetables and fruit. There were boxes with broken jars of jelly and salad dressing. Other boxes had stale bread and cookie crumbs.

And here, behind the supermarket, lived Mother Mouse. One day while poking around in the trash pile looking for treasures for her mouse nest, she found a crushed box of Neat-O Bubble Bath. Mother Mouse loved the way the bubble bath smelled. She thought it was the sweetest smell in all the world!

When her son was born, Mother Mouse named him Neat-O
and used an empty bubble bath box for his bed. Neat-O
loved the smell of the bubble bath box. It made him smile.

One day Mother Mouse put Neat-O in his bed and set it out in the warm sunshine. While Neat-O was asleep, dark clouds covered the sun. Raindrops began to fall into the box—plop, plop, plop. The rain mixed with the bubble bath still in the box, and bubbles began to pop up! Soon Neat-O was covered with bubbles!

Neat-O woke up with bubbles all around him. The bubbles tickled his nose.

Mother Mouse came running to take him inside. She thought Neat-O would be crying, but he wasn't. Instead, he was laughing. He loved the bubbles.

After that Neat-O wanted a bubble bath every day. He liked the smell of bubbles and the way they tickled his nose.

Neat-O grew fast and always smelled good . . . just like Neat-O Bubble Bath.

The rowdy rats made fun of Neat-O. They teased him about taking bubble baths.

The biggest one, Ratty, called out, "Look at that sweet-smelling mouse!"

Rough Rat said, "There goes the bathing beauty!" It was very embarrassing for Neat-O.

Neat-O thought, "Maybe I shouldn't take bubble baths. Maybe I shouldn't take any kind of baths. Maybe I should stay dirty. Then the rats would stop teasing me."

The next morning he did not take a bubble bath. His fur did not look so soft, but no one seemed to notice except Mother Mouse. She said to herself, "I guess Neat-O forgot."

The day after that Neat-O did not take a bath. His fur did not look soft and smooth at all. It began to look a little scruffy. He grinned to himself, "Now, no one will tease me about being too clean and sweet smelling."

For a week or so Mother Mouse kept hoping Neat-O would decide to be neat and clean again, but he didn't. He went right on getting dirtier and dirtier.

After the second week Neat-O began to notice something. When he went near anyone, that mouse would move away.

No one wanted to be near him. No one would talk to him. When he met his mother's friends, they would hold their noses and run.

Being dirty like the rowdy rats was not much fun. But Neat-O couldn't give up now. He was determined to be like the gang.

Mother Mouse was determined too. She said to herself, "This has gone far enough. If Neat-O is not going to take a bath, then I will give him one."

Neat-O noticed his mother looking at him. The look on her face worried him. He really got worried when she frowned and started walking toward him. He started to run!

Neat-O ran and ran. When he stopped and looked back, his mother was no longer behind him. In fact, he didn't see her anywhere. "Ah-ha!" he said. "She knew she couldn't catch me."

He danced a funny little dance and stumbled right into a carton of rotten eggs! The eggs broke and Neat-O was covered from head to toe. He coughed and spluttered and tried to wipe the awful stuff out of his eyes.

Neat-O couldn't see where he was going. He ran into a box of spoiled broccoli and cabbages. They smelled almost as bad as the eggs.

At that moment, who should come by but Ratty, the biggest bully rat in the neighborhood. Neat-O said, "Hello there, friend." The rat took a look, whiffed a whiff, and said, "You've been in our garbage!" He whiffed another whiff and moved back.

Rough Rat walked up, saying, "If we catch you in our garbage again, you'll be sorry." He sniffed a sniff of the little mouse and started going around in dizzy circles. He grabbed onto his friend and said, "Hey, Ratty, do we smell like that?"

"If we do," said Ratty, "I think we had better take baths. Come on, Rough Rat." Off they ran, leaving the little mouse standing there all alone.

Neat-O was beginning to wonder if being dirty was such a good idea after all. Suddenly someone jumped out from behind a carton and grabbed him.

Neat-O cried, "Help! Help!" Then he saw it was his mother. Mother Mouse said, "Young Mouse, you're coming straight home with me!" She held him by one ear, which was the cleanest part of him, and marched him home to the mouse nest.

Mother Mouse filled the bathtub with warm water and bubble bath and plopped Neat-O in the bath. He wanted to kick and fuss, but the warm water did feel good. Neat-O snuggled down in the bubbles. He felt so drowsy that he could almost fall asleep.

But no!—Mother Mouse sat him up straight and picked up her scrubbing brush.

"Your fur is a mess," she said. "It needs a good scrubbing!" Neat-O squirmed and wiggled. The brush didn't feel too good.

Mother Mouse lifted Neat-O out of the tub and sat him on a cracker box. "Look how dirty this bath water is!" she said. She poured the dirty water down the drain and rinsed out the tub.

"Thank goodness the bath is over," said Neat-O.

"Not yet," said his mother. She put bubble bath in the tub and filled it up again with warm water.

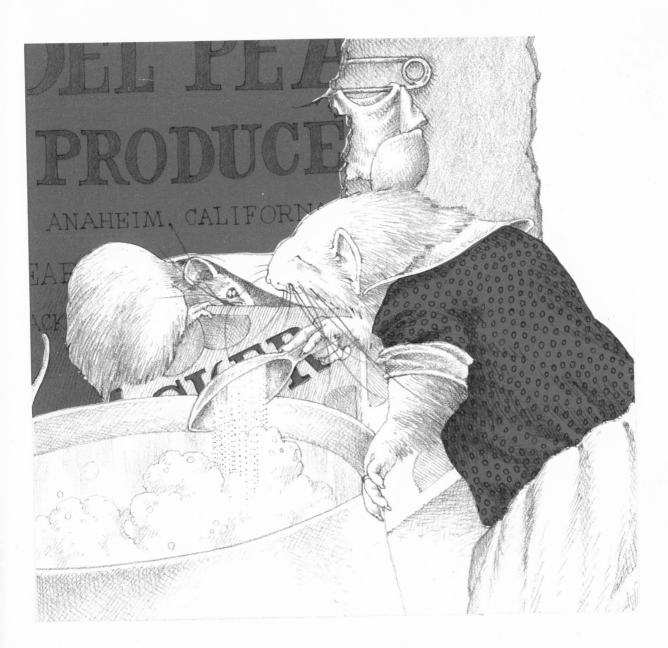

She put Neat-O back in the tub, and soon he nestled down in the bubbles and grinned.

Neat-O felt like himself again—the little mouse who really enjoyed taking baths and feeling clean.